The Adventures of Cheze and Kwackers

Book 2

Jonah and the Whale
and

Daniel in the Lion's Den

by Bobby Goldsboro

Illustrated by Toni Donelow Stewart

New Canaan Publishing Company Inc.
New Canaan, Connecticut, USA.

10 9 8 7 6 5 4 3 2 1

ISBN 1-889658-28-6

Library of Congress Cataloging-in-Publication Data

Goldsboro, Bobby.
   Jonah and the whale ; and, Daniel in the lion's den / by Bobby Goldsboro ; illustrated by Toni Donelow Stewart.
        p. cm. — (Bobby Goldsboro's The adventures of Cheze and Kwackers ; Book 2)
Summary: A duck named Kwackers tells two Old Testament stories to his friend, a scruffy little mouse named Cheze, and explains what they teach about faith, trust, and obedience.
   ISBN 1-889658-28-6 (pbk.)
   1. Jonah (Biblical prophet)—Juvenile fiction. 2. Daniel (Biblical character)—Juvenile fiction. [1. Jonah (Biblical prophet)—Fiction. 2. Daniel (Biblical character)—Fiction. 3. Cats—Fiction. 4. Mice—Fiction. 5. Conduct of life—Fiction.] I. Title: Jonah and the whale, and, Daniel in the lion's den. II. Title: Johah and the whale. III. Title: Daniel in the lion's den. IV. Stewart, Toni Donelow, ill. V. Title. VI. Series.
   PZ7.G56995 Jo 2002
   [Fic]—dc21
                                                                2002009204

1. Jonah and the Whale

One Sunday, Cheze was down at the pond visiting his friend, Kwackers. Cheze was sitting next to the water's edge. "Boy, it must be nice living on the water," said Cheze. "You don't have to worry about being stepped on or eaten by a cat!"

"Well, there are just as many dangers out here in the pond," said Kwackers.

"Aw, what kind of danger could there be out there?" asked Cheze.

Suddenly, a huge bass fish leaped out of the water and lunged at Cheze. Cheze jumped away from the water's edge just in time. The big fish disappeared into the water.

"Wow, any closer and that fish would have swallowed me!" said Cheze. "That would have been the end of me!"

"Where's your faith?" asked Kwackers. "Jonah still had faith in the Lord, even when he was swallowed up by a whale!"

"You mean someone was swallowed up by a whale and lived to tell about it?" asked Cheze.

"That's right," said Kwackers. "Jonah trusted in the Lord, and he was saved."

Then Cheze said, "Well, what was this Jonah doing in the whale's mouth to begin with?"

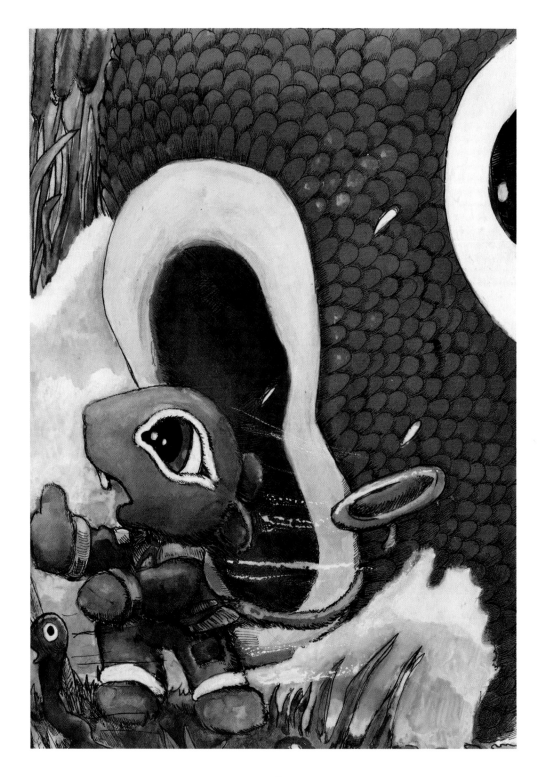

"Well, he started out in a boat," said Kwackers. "You see, there was once a great city named Nineveh. But the people who lived there had become wicked and sinful. So God called on Jonah to go to Nineveh and tell the people to change their wicked ways. And if they didn't, then God was going to destroy Nineveh and everyone who lived there.

Jonah started out on his journey, but then he started thinking. What if the people of Nineveh didn't believe him? What if they thought he was lying? What would they do to him?"

"Jonah decided to look for a ship he could board to sail away from Nineveh. He was afraid to go there. Jonah thought he could hide from God."

"I'll sail far out to sea, and God won't know where I am. Then I won't have to go to Nineveh," said Cheze, acting like Jonah.

"Jonah found a ship and asked the crew if he could sail with them," Kwackers continued. 'I know you,' said the captain. 'You're Jonah, the one who talks to God. If you sail with us, we'll have good weather. Come aboard.' So Jonah boarded the ship. He didn't tell the crew that he was trying to hide from God."

"Once the ship was far out to sea, the sky grew darker. The winds started blowing hard. The waves got bigger and bigger. Suddenly, the ship was in the middle of a huge storm. Jonah ran downstairs to hide inside the boat. The ship's crew tried to get the ship back to shore, but the storm was too fierce. The little boat was being tossed around and was in danger of sinking."

"The ship's captain ran down to Jonah. 'Jonah,' said the captain, 'You are the one who speaks to God. You can help us. You must pray to your God to save us.'"

"But Jonah said, 'It is my fault that the storm has come. God asked me to do something for Him, and I disobeyed. We are all being punished for something that I did. The only way to calm the storm is to throw me overboard, into the sea!' The captain did not want to throw Jonah into the sea, so he kept trying to sail to safety. But it was of no use."

"Finally, the captain and the crew knew that Jonah was right. The only way to keep the ship from sinking was to throw Jonah overboard. So they grabbed Jonah and threw him into the sea!"

"The sea suddenly became calm, and the winds died down. The storm was over. Now the storm had shown Jonah the power of God, but Jonah was about to learn about God's forgiveness and God's love as well."

"As Jonah sank down into the sea, he thought his life was over. Then suddenly, a huge fish appeared. The fish looked at Jonah, opened its mouth, and swallowed Jonah whole! Jonah opened his eyes and realized that he was inside the fish's belly. 'God, you have saved me,' said Jonah. 'I disobeyed you, yet you showed me forgiveness.'"

"The crew of the ship made it back to shore, and they told everyone what had happened. The people of Nineveh heard that Jonah had been swallowed by a whale. But all the time Jonah was in the belly of that huge fish, he never gave up hope. He knew that God was watching out for him. Finally, after three days, the big fish spat Jonah out onto the shore. Jonah was on dry land, safe and sound. Jonah then told God that he would go to Nineveh and warn the people, just as God had commanded."

"When the people of Nineveh saw Jonah, they couldn't believe it! He was supposed to have died at sea. Why, the crew had even seen him swallowed by a great fish!"

"Jonah explained what had happened. God had shown His power as well as His love. When the people of Nineveh heard this, they were afraid, and immediately they changed their sinful ways. The city of Nineveh was saved, and the people once again obeyed God's laws. Jonah had been swallowed by a big fish, and he had lived to tell about it, thanks to God's love."

"Cheze, wake up!" Kwackers continued. "I can't believe you fell asleep. You didn't even hear the story of Jonah and the whale."

"Jonah and the whale? Why sure I did," said Cheze. "But it wasn't a whale, it was a bass. And it was I, not Jonah, who got swallowed up."

"And I was thrown into the ocean and sank to the bottom! But the fish swallowed me up. And I lived in his stomach for three whole days! And it didn't smell too good in there! Why did that old fish have to swallow me?"

"Well, if the fish hadn't swallowed you, I mean, swallowed Jonah, Jonah would have drowned. God told the fish to swallow Jonah to save him. But Jonah also had to prove his love for God. That's why he stayed in the fish's stomach for three long days. Jonah kept his faith, and God spared him."

"Say, Kwackers, why didn't Jonah just go to Nineveh in the first place?" Cheze asked his friend. "He wouldn't have had to go to sea, and he wouldn't have been swallowed by the fish!"

"Well, Cheze, it isn't always easy to do the things God wants us to do," Kwackers replied. "Sometimes it's easier just to run away and hide, like Jonah tried to do. But if you trust in God and obey His commandments, He'll watch out for you."

"Boy, what a great story! And that story is in the Bible?" Cheze asked.

It sure is," Kwackers replied. "And lots more just like it. The most exciting stories you'll ever read are right there in the Bible."

"Well, that story taught me a lot. There's danger out there no matter where you live. But if you trust in God, he'll protect you," said Cheze.

"That's right, Cheze. But you also have to use common sense. In other words, don't stand next to the water if there's something in there that could eat you! You also have to protect yourself!"

"I learned my lesson, Kwackers," said Cheze. Well, I had better get going. I'll see you next Sunday for another Bible lesson. So long!"

2. Daniel in the Lion's Den

It was still early in the morning, but it was already hot. Kwackers was splashing around in the pond. "This cool water sure feels good," he said. "On days like this, I'm really glad to be a duck!"

Then Kwackers heard a voice. "Well, *I'm not* a duck! So how about splashing some of that water my way?" Kwackers looked around, and there was his little mouse friend, Cheze, almost out of breath.

"I just ran all the way over here, and I'm thirsty," said Cheze.

"Why didn't you walk over?" asked Kwackers.

"Because there's an alley full of cats back there," said Cheze. "I was surrounded by millions of cats!"

"Millions?" said Kwackers.

"Well, there were more than two of them," said Cheze. "I barely got away!" Cheze took off his cap, dipped it into the water, and began to drink from it. "Nobody knows what it's like to be surrounded by big cats," said Cheze.

"Oh, Daniel knew what it was like," said Kwackers. "But he had God with him. It looks like God was with you this morning, too!"

"Who was Daniel?" asked Cheze. "Was he someone in the Bible?"

"He sure was," said Kwackers. "Daniel was surrounded by bigger cats than you were. Actually, he was surrounded by lions!"

"Lions?" said Cheze, as he climbed up on a toadstool. "Where was Daniel? At the zoo?"

"Oh, no," said Kwackers. "This story took place long, long ago in a place called Babylonia."

"Baba. .whatia?" asked Cheze.

"Babylonia," said Kwackers. "You see, back then there was a king named Nebuchadnezzar who kept the people of Israel as captives. The king chose the smartest young people from Israel and educated them."

"Because Daniel and the other young people of Israel had obeyed God's laws, they were blessed with great wisdom. Daniel had been given the ability to understand dreams. Now, the king had begun to have bad dreams, and he could not understand them. He called his magicians and said, 'Tell me the meaning of my dreams.' When they could not do this, the king ordered Daniel to put the magicians to death. Daniel did not want to see the magicians harmed, so he prayed to God for guidance. That night God came to Daniel in a vision, and God told Daniel what to do."

"The next day, Daniel went to see the king. Daniel told the king that only God could tell the meaning of his dreams. Then Daniel told the king what God had told him in a vision. God had told him that the king's dreams were about the future. God had said that no matter how great Nebuchadnezzar's kingdom became, it would one day be destroyed, just as other kingdoms had been. After all, the kingdoms on earth were made of stone, iron, and clay. But God's kingdom would never be destroyed."

"The king was so impressed with Daniel that he spared the lives of the magicians. He made Daniel the chief over all the wise men of Babylonia."

"When Nebuchadnezzar died, his son became king. The son gave Daniel even more power over the other wise men. Later, when the son died, a man named Darius became king. Darius honored Daniel above all others. He even planned on making Daniel the ruler of the kingdom some day."

"But this only made all the other wise men jealous of Daniel. Since Daniel was an honest man and obeyed God's laws, they could not find fault with him. So they decided to trick king Darius."

"The wise men went to the king and advised him that he should order all the people of his kingdom to worship only him for thirty days. That would strengthen his power over his people. King Darius thought this was a good idea. So king Darius ordered everyone to worship only him for thirty days. Anyone who didn't do so would be thrown into the lion's den."

"Then the wise men went to watch Daniel. They knew he would still worship God. They watched Daniel pray to God three times, just as he did every day."

"The wise men went straight to king Darius. 'Daniel did not obey your command,' said the wise men. 'He worshipped his God instead of you. He must be thrown to the lions!'"

"King Darius had been tricked by the wise men. He did not want to throw Daniel to the lions, but he had to. So king Darius said to Daniel, 'May you be saved by the God that you pray to.'"

"Daniel was arrested and taken away. He was thrown into the lion's den. Suddenly, the lions came into the den and surrounded Daniel. Then a huge rock was placed at the entrance of the den so that Daniel could not escape. But Daniel was not afraid. He knew that God would keep him safe."

"That night, the king could not sleep. Early the next morning, the king ran to the lion's den. He cried out, 'Daniel, did your God save you?' Daniel answered, 'I am safe, my king. God sent an angel to keep the mouths of the lions shut. They did not harm me.'"

"The stone was removed, and Daniel walked out, safe and sound. The king then said, 'your God is truly the God above all, and only His kingdom will last forever!' So you see, Cheze, Daniel's faith in God kept him from being eaten by the lions," said Kwackers.

"Wow, after being surrounded by lions, those cats don't seem scary at all!" said Cheze. "But what happened to the men who tricked the king?"

"Well," said Kwackers, "the king had them thrown into the lion's den because of what they had done. And since they had not obeyed God's laws, they were not saved!"

45

"You know," said Cheze, "it seems pretty simple. If we just obey God's laws and act like we're supposed to, we'll be okay."

"That's right," said Kwackers. "But sometimes that's easier said than done."

"What do you mean?" asked Cheze.

"Well, sometimes we're tempted by friends or even strangers to do something that we know to be wrong," said Kwackers. "And sometimes it's harder to do the right thing than the wrong thing. That's when you just have to ask yourself, 'What would God want me to do?'"

"So even if it makes your friends angry, or it makes them laugh at you, you still have to do the right thing," said Kwackers. "After all, you want to go to heaven, don't you?"

"I sure do," said Cheze. "Then I won't have to worry about any old cats!"

Kwackers laughed and said, "I'm sure there are cats in heaven, too. But the only ones you have to worry about are here on earth. Just be careful, obey God's laws, and you'll be okay."

"Thanks, Kwackers," said Cheze as he walked away. "See you next Sunday."